MED SHIP MAN

MED SHIP MAN

by Murray Leinster

Calhoun regarded the communicator with something like exasperation as his taped voice repeated a standard approach-call for the twentieth time. But no answer came, which had become irritating a long time ago. This was a new Med Service sector for Calhoun. He'd been assigned to another man's tour of duty because the other man had been taken down with romance. He'd gotten married, which ruled him out for Med Ship duty. So now Calhoun listened to his own voice endlessly repeating a call that should have been answered immediately.

Murgatroyd the *tormal* watched with beady, interested eyes. The planet Maya lay off to port of the Med Ship *Esclipus Twenty*. Its almost circular disk showed full size on a vision screen beside the ship's control board. The image was absolutely clear and vividly colored. There was an ice cap in view. There were continents. There were seas. The cloud system of a considerable cyclonic disturbance could be noted off at one side, and the continents looked reasonably as they should, and the seas were of that muddy, indescribable tint which indicates deep water.

Calhoun's own voice, taped an hour earlier, sounded in a speaker as it went again to the communicator and then to the extremely visible world a hundred thousand miles away.

"*Calling ground,*" said Calhoun's recorded voice. "*Med Ship* Esclipus Twenty *calling ground to report arrival and ask coordinates for landing. Our mass is fifty standard tons. Repeat, five-oh tons. Purpose of landing, planetary health inspection.*"

*

The recorded voice stopped. There was silence except for the taped random noises which kept the inside of the ship from feeling like the inside of a tomb.

Murgatroyd said: "*Chee?*"

Calhoun said ironically, "Undoubtedly, Murgatroyd. Undoubtedly! Whoever's on duty at the spaceport stepped out for a moment, or dropped dead, or did something equally inconvenient. We have to wait until he gets back or somebody else takes over."

Murgatroyd said "*Chee!*" again and began to lick his whiskers. He knew that when Calhoun called on the communicator, another human voice should reply. Then there should be conversation, and shortly the force-fields of a landing-grid should take hold of the Med Ship and draw it planet-ward. In time it ought to touch ground in a spaceport with a gigantic, silvery landing-grid rising skyward all about it. Then there should be people greeting Calhoun cordially and welcoming Murgatroyd with smiles and petting.

"*Calling ground*," said the recorded voice yet again. "*Med Ship* Esclipus Twenty—"

It went on through the formal notice of arrival. Murgatroyd waited in pleasurable anticipation. When the Med Ship arrived at a port of call humans gave him sweets and cakes, and they thought it charming that he drank coffee just like a human, only with more gusto. Aground, Murgatroyd moved zestfully in society while Calhoun worked. Calhoun's work was conferences with planetary health officials, politely receiving such information as they thought important, and tactfully telling them about the most recent developments in medical science as known to the Interstellar Medical Service.

"Somebody," said Calhoun darkly, "is going to catch the devil for this!"

The communicator loudspeaker spoke abruptly.

"Calling Med Ship," said a voice. "Calling Med Ship *Esclipus Twenty!* Liner *Candida* calling. Have you had an answer from ground?"

Calhoun blinked. Then he said curtly:

"Not yet. I've been calling all of half an hour, and never a word out of them!"

"We've been in orbit twelve hours," said the voice from emptiness. "Calling all the while. No answer. We don't like it."

Calhoun flipped a switch that threw a vision screen into circuit with the ship's electron telescope. A starfield appeared and shifted wildly. Then a bright dot centered itself. He raised the magnification. The bright dot swelled and became a chubby commercial ship, with the false ports that passengers like to believe they looked through when in space. Two relatively large cargo ports on each side showed that it carried heavy freight in addition to passengers. It was one of those workhorse intra-cluster ships that distributed the freight and passengers the long-haul liners dumped off only at established transshipping ports.

Murgatroyd padded across the Med Ship's cabin and examined the image with a fine air of wisdom. It did not mean anything to him, but *tormals* imitate human actions as parrots and parrakeets imitate human speech. He said, "*Chee!*" as if making an observation of profound significance, then went back to the cushion and again curled up.

"We don't see anything wrong aground," the liner's voice complained, "but they don't answer calls! We don't get any scatter-signals either. We went down to two diameters and couldn't pick up a thing. And we have a passenger to land. He insists on it!"

*

By ordinary, communications between different places on a planet's surface use frequencies the ion-layers of the atmosphere either reflect or refract down past the horizon. But there is usually some small leakage to space, and line-of-sight frequencies are generally abundant. It is one of the annoyances of a ship coming in to port that space near most planets is usually full of local signals.

"I'll check," said Calhoun curtly. "Stand by."

The *Candida* would have arrived off Maya as the Med Ship had done, and called down as Calhoun had been doing. It was very probably a ship on schedule and the grid operator at the spaceport should have expected it. Space commerce was important to any planet, comparing more or less with the export-import business of an industrial nation in ancient times on Earth. Planets had elaborate traffic-aid systems for the cargo-carriers which moved between solar systems as they'd once moved between continents on Earth. Such traffic aids were very carefully maintained. Certainly for a spaceport landing-grid not to respond to calls for twelve hours running seemed ominous.

"We've been wondering," said the *Candida* querulously, "if there could be something radically wrong below. Sickness, for example."

The word "sickness" was a substitute for a more alarming word. But a plague had nearly wiped out the population of Dorset, once upon a time, and the first ships to arrive after it had broken out most incautiously went down to ground, and so carried the plague to their next two ports of call. Nowadays quarantine regulations were enforced very strictly indeed.

"I'll try to find out what's the matter," said Calhoun.

"We've got a passenger," repeated the *Candida* aggrievedly, "who insists that we land him by space-boat if we don't make a ship landing. He says he has important business aground."

7

Calhoun did not answer. The rights of passengers were extravagantly protected, these days. To fail to deliver a passenger to his destination entitled him to punitive damages which no spaceline could afford. So the Med Ship would seem heaven-sent to the *Candida*'s skipper. Calhoun could relieve him of responsibility.

The telescope screen winked and showed the surface of the planet a hundred thousand miles away. Calhoun glared at the image on the port screen and guided the telescope to the spaceport city—Maya City. He saw highways and blocks of buildings. He saw the spaceport and its landing-grid. He could see no motion, of course.

He raised the magnification. He raised it again. Still no motion. He upped the magnification until the lattice-pattern of the telescope's amplifying crystal began to show. But at the ship's distance from the planet, a ground-car would represent only the fortieth of a second of arc. There was atmosphere, too, with thermals; anything the size of a ground-car simply couldn't be seen.

But the city showed quite clearly. Nothing massive had happened to it. No large-scale physical disaster had occurred. It simply did not answer calls from space.

*

Calhoun flipped off the screen.

"I think," he said irritably into the communicator microphone, "I suspect I'll have to make an emergency landing. It could be something as trivial as a power failure—" but he knew that was wildly improbable—"or it could be—anything. I'll land on rockets and tell you what I find."

The voice from the *Candida* said hopefully:

"Can you authorize us to refuse to land our passenger for his own protection? He's raising the devil! He insists that his business demands that he be landed."

A word from Calhoun as a Med Service man would protect the spaceliner from a claim for damages. But Calhoun didn't like the look of things. He realized, distastefully, that he might find practically anything down below. He might find that he had to quarantine the planet and himself with it. In such a case he'd need the *Candida* to carry word of the quarantine to other planets and thus to Med Service sector headquarters.

"We've lost a lot of time," insisted the *Candida*. "Can you authorize us—"

"Not yet," said Calhoun. "I'll tell you when I land."

"But—"

"I'm signing off for the moment," said Calhoun. "Stand by."

He headed the little ship downward, and as it gathered velocity he went over the briefing sheets covering this particular world. He'd never touched ground here before. His occupation, of course, was seeing to the dissemination of medical science as it developed under the Med Service. The Service itself was neither political nor administrative. But it was important. Every human-occupied world was supposed to have a Med Ship visit at least once in four years to verify the state of public health.

Med Ship men like Calhoun offered advice on public-health problems. When something out of the ordinary turned up, the Med Service had a staff of researchers who hadn't been wholly baffled yet. There were great ships which could carry the ultimate in laboratory equipment and specialized personnel to any place where they were needed. Not less than a dozen inhabited worlds in this sector alone owed the survival of their populations to the Med Service, and the number of those which couldn't have been colonized without Med Service help was legion.

Calhoun reread the briefing. Maya was one of four planets in this general area whose life systems seemed to have had a common origin, suggesting that the Arrhenius theory of space-traveling spores was true in some limited sense. A genus of ground-cover plants with motile stems and leaves and cannibalistic tendencies was considered strong evidence of common origin.

The planet had been colonized for two centuries now, and produced organic compounds of great value from indigenous plants, most of which were used in textile manufacture. There were no local endemic infections to which men were susceptible. A number of human-use crops were grown. Cereals, grasses and grains, however, could not be grown because of the native ground-cover motile-stem plants. All wheat and cereal food had to be imported, which fact severely limited Maya's population. There were about two million people on the planet, settled on a peninsula in the Yucatan Sea and a small area of mainland. Public-health surveys had shown a great many things about a great many subjects ... but there was no mention of anything to account for the failure of the spaceport to respond to arrival calls from space. Naturally!

The Med Ship drove on down, and the planet revolved beneath it.

As Maya's sunlit hemisphere enlarged, Calhoun kept the telescope's field wide. He saw cities, and vast areas of cleared land where native plants were grown as raw materials for the organics' manufactures. He saw very little true chlorophyll green, though. Mayan foliage tended to a dark olive color.

*

At fifty miles he was sure that the city streets were empty even of ground-car traffic. There was no spaceship aground in the landing-grid. There were no ground-cars in motion on the splendid, multiple-lane highways.

At thirty miles altitude there were still no signals in the atmosphere, though when he tried amplitude-modulation reception he picked up static. But there was no normally modulated signal on the air at any frequency. At twenty miles—no. At fifteen miles, broadcast power was available, which proved that the landing-grid was working as usual, tapping the upper atmosphere for electric charges to furnish power for all the planet's needs.

From ten miles down to ground-touch, Calhoun was busy.

It is not too difficult to land a ship on rockets, with reasonably level ground to land on. But landing at a specific spot is something else. Calhoun juggled the ship to descend inside the grid itself. His rockets burned out pencil-thin holes through the clay and stone beneath the tarmac. He cut them off.

Silence. Stillness. The Med Ship's outside microphones picked up small noises of wind blowing over the city. There was no other sound at all.

—No. There was a singularly deliberate clicking sound, not loud and not fast. Perhaps a click—a double click—every two seconds. That was all.

Calhoun went into the airlock, with Murgatroyd frisking a little in the expectation of great social success among the people of this world. When Calhoun cracked the outer airlock door he smelled something. It was a faintly sour, astringent odor that had the quality of decay in it. But it was no kind of decay he recognized. Again stillness and silence. No traffic-noise; not even the almost inaudible murmur that every city has in all its ways at all hours. The buildings looked as buildings should look at daybreak, except that the doors and windows were open. It was somehow shocking.

A ruined city is dramatic. An abandoned city is pathetic. This was neither. It was something new. It felt as if everybody had walked away, out of sight, within the past few minutes.

Calhoun headed for the spaceport building with Murgatroyd ambling puzzledly at his side. Murgatroyd was disturbed. There should be people here! They should welcome Calhoun and admire him—Murgatroyd—and he should be a social lion with all the sweets he could eat and all the coffee he could put into his expandable belly. But nothing happened! Nothing at all.

"*Chee?*" he asked anxiously.

"They've gone away," growled Calhoun. "They probably left in ground-cars. There's not one in sight."

There wasn't. Calhoun could look out through the grid foundations and see long, sunlit and absolutely empty streets. He arrived at the spaceport building. There was—there had been—a green area about the base of the structure. There was not a living plant left. Leaves were wilted and limp. The remains had become almost a jelly of collapsed stems and blossoms of dark olive-green. The plants were dead; but not long enough to have dried up. They might have wilted two or three days before.

Calhoun went in the building. The spaceport log lay open on a desk. It recorded the arrival of freight to be shipped away—undoubtedly—on the *Candida* now uneasily in orbit somewhere aloft. There was no sign of disorder. It was exactly as if the people here had walked out to look at something interesting, and hadn't come back.

Calhoun trudged out of the spaceport and to the streets and buildings of the city proper. It was incredible! Doors were opened or unlocked. Merchandise in the shops lay on display, exactly as it had been spread out to interest customers. There was no sign of confusion anywhere. Even in a restaurant there were dishes and flatware on the tables. The food in the plates was stale, as if three days old, but it hadn't yet begun to spoil. The appearance of everything was as if people at their meals had simply, at some signal, gotten up and walked out without any panic or disturbance.

Calhoun made a wry face. He'd remembered something. Among the tales that had been carried from Earth to the other worlds of the galaxy there was a completely unimportant mystery story which people still sometimes tried to write an ending to. It was the story of an ancient sailing ship called the *Marie Celeste*, which was found drifting aimlessly in the middle of the ocean. There was food on the cabin table, and the galley stove was still warm. There was no sign of any trouble, or terror, or disturbance which might cause the ship to be abandoned. But there was not a living soul on board. Nobody had ever been able to contrive a believable explanation.

"Only," said Calhoun to Murgatroyd, "this is on a larger scale. The people of this city walked out about three days ago, and didn't come back. Maybe all the people on the planet did the same, since there's not a communicator in operation anywhere. To make the understatement of the century, Murgatroyd, I don't like this. I don't like it a bit!"

II

On the way back to the Med Ship, Calhoun stopped at another place where, on a grass-growing planet, there would have been green sward. There were Earth-type trees, and some native ones, and between them there should have been a lawn. The trees were thriving, but the ground-cover plants were collapsed and rotting.

Calhoun picked up a bit of the semi-slime and smelled it. It was faintly sour, astringent, the same smell he'd noticed when he opened the airlock door. He threw the stuff away and brushed off his hands. Something had killed the ground-cover plants which had the habit of killing Earth-type grass when planted here.

He listened. Everywhere that humans live, there are insects and birds and other tiny creatures which are essential parts of the ecological system to which the human race is adjusted. They have to be carried to and established upon every new world that mankind hopes to occupy. But there was no sound of such living creatures here.

It was probable that the bellowing roar of the Med Ship's emergency rockets was the only real noise the city had heard since its people went away.

The stillness bothered Murgatroyd. He said, "*Chee!*" in a subdued tone and stayed close to Calhoun. Calhoun shook his head. Then he said abruptly:

"Come along, Murgatroyd!"

He went back to the building housing the grid controls. He didn't look at the spaceport log this time. He went to the instruments recording the second function of a landing-grid. In addition to lifting up and letting down ships of space, a landing-grid drew down power from the ions of the upper atmosphere and broadcast it. It provided all the energy that humans on a world could need. It was solar power, in a way, absorbed and stored by a layer of ions miles high, which then could be drawn on and distributed by the grid. During his descent Calhoun had noted that broadcast power was still available. Now he looked at what the instruments said.

The needle on the dial showing power-drain moved slowly back and forth. It was a rhythmic movement, going from maximum to minimum power-use, and then back again. Approximately six million kilowatts was being taken out of the broadcast every two seconds for half of one second. Then the drain cut off for a second and a half, and went on again for half a second.

Frowning, Calhoun raised his eyes to a very fine color photograph on the wall above the power dials. It was a picture of the human-occupied part of Maya, taken four thousand miles out in space. It had been enlarged to four feet by six, and Maya City could be seen as an irregular group of squares and triangles measuring a little more than half an inch by three-quarters. The detail was perfect. It was possible to see perfectly straight, infinitely thin lines moving out from the city. They were multiple-lane highways, mathematically straight from one city to another, and then mathematically straight—though at a new angle—until the next. Calhoun stared thoughtfully at them.

"The people left the city in a hurry," he told Murgatroyd, "and there was little confusion, if any. So they knew in advance that they might have to go. They were ready for it. If they took anything, they had it ready packed in their cars. But they hadn't been sure they'd have to go because they were going about their businesses as usual. All the shops were open and people were eating in restaurants, and so on."

Murgatroyd said, "*Chee!*" as if in full agreement.

"Now," demanded Calhoun, "where did they go? The question's really where could they go! There were about eight hundred thousand people in this city. There'd be cars for everyone, of course, and two hundred thousand cars would take everybody. But that's a lot of ground-cars! Put 'em two hundred feet apart on a highway, and that's twenty-six cars to the mile on each lane. Run them at a hundred miles an hour on a twelve-lane road—using all lanes one way—and that's twenty-six hundred cars per lane per hour, and that's thirty-one thousand ... two highways make sixty-two ... three highways.... With two highways they could empty the city in under three hours, and with three highways close to two. Since there's no sign of panic, that's what they must have done. Must have worked it out in advance, too. Maybe they'd done it before it happened ... whatever it was that happened."

*

He searched the photograph which was so much more detailed than a map. There were mountains to the north of Maya City, but only one highway led north. There were more mountains to the west. One highway went into them, but not through. To the south there was sea, which curved around some three hundred miles from Maya City and put the human colony on Maya on a peninsula.

"They went east," said Calhoun presently. He traced lines with his finger. "Three highways go east; that's the only way they could go quickly. They hadn't been sure they'd have to go but they knew where to go when they did. So when they got their warning, they left. On three highways, to the east. And we'll follow them and ask what the hell they ran away from. Nothing's visible here!"

He went back to the Med Ship, Murgatroyd skipping with him.

As the airlock door closed behind them, he heard a click from the outside-microphone speakers. He listened. It was a doubled clicking, as of something turned on and almost at once turned off again. There was a two-second cycle, the same as that of the power drain. Something drawing six million kilowatts went on and immediately off again every two seconds. It made a sound in speakers linked to outside microphones, but it didn't make a noise in the air. The microphone clicks were induction; pick-up; like cross-talk on defective telephone cables.

Calhoun shrugged his shoulders almost up to his ears. He went to the communicator.

"Calling *Candida*—" he began, and the answer almost leaped down his throat.

"*Candida* to Med Ship. Come in! Come in! What's happened down there?"

"The city's deserted without any sign of panic," said Calhoun, "and there's power and nothing seems to be broken down. But it's as if somebody had said, 'Everybody clear out' and they did. That doesn't happen on a whim! What's your next port of call?"

The *Candida*'s voice told him, hopefully.

"Take a report," commanded Calhoun. "Deliver it to the public health office immediately you land. They'll get it to Med Service sector headquarters. I'm going to stay here and find out what's been going on."

He dictated, growing irritated as he did so because he couldn't explain what he reported. Something serious had taken place, but there was no clue as to what it was. Strictly speaking, it wasn't certainly a public health affair. But any emergency the size of this one involved public health factors.

"I'm remaining aground to investigate," finished Calhoun. "I will report further when or if it is possible. Message ends."

"What about our passenger?"

"To the devil with your passenger!" said Calhoun peevishly. "Do as you please!"

*

He cut off the communicator and prepared for activity outside the ship. Presently he and Murgatroyd went to look for transportation. The Med Ship couldn't be used for a search operation; it didn't carry enough rocket fuel. They'd have to use a ground vehicle.

It was again shocking to note that nothing had moved but sun shadows. Again it seemed that everybody had simply walked out of some door or other and failed to come back. Calhoun saw the windows of jewelers' shops. Treasures lay unguarded in plain view. He saw a florist's shop. Here there were Earth-type flowers apparently thriving, and some strange beautiful flowers with olive-green foliage which throve as well as the Earth-plants. There was a cage in which a plant had grown, and that plant was wilting and about to rot. But a plant that had to be grown in a cage....

He found a ground-car agency, perhaps for imported cars, perhaps for those built on Maya. He went in and from the cars on display he chose one, an elaborate sports car. He turned its key and it hummed. He drove it carefully out into the empty street, Murgatroyd sitting interestedly beside him.

"This is luxury, Murgatroyd," said Calhoun. "Also it's grand theft. We medical characters can't usually afford such things. Or have an excuse to steal them. But these are parlous times, so we take a chance."

"*Chee!*" said Murgatroyd.

"We want to find a fugitive population and ask what they ran away from. As of the moment, it seems that they ran away from nothing. They may be pleased to know they can come back."

Murgatroyd again said, "*Chee!*"

Calhoun drove through vacant ways. It was somehow nerve-racking. He felt as if someone should pop out and say "Boo!" at any instant. He discovered an elevated highway and a ramp leading up to it. At a cloverleaf he drove eastward, watching sharply for any sign of life. There was none.

He was nearly out of the city when he felt the chest impact of a sonic boom, and then heard a trailing away growling sound which seemed to come from farther away as it died out. It was the result of something traveling faster than sound, so that the noise it made far away had to catch up with the sound it emitted nearby.

He stared up. He saw a parachute blossom as a bare speck against the blue. Then he heard the even deeper-toned roaring of a supersonic craft climbing skyward. It could be a spaceliner's lifeboat, descended into atmosphere and going out again.

It was. It had left a parachute behind, and now went back to space to rendezvous with its parent ship.

"That," said Calhoun impatiently, "will be the *Candida*'s passenger. He was insistent enough."

He scowled. The *Candida*'s voice had said its passenger demanded to be landed for business reasons. And Calhoun had a prejudice against some kinds of business men who would think their own affairs more important than anything else. Two standard years before, he'd made a planetary health inspection on Texia II, in another galactic sector. It was a llano planet and a single giant business enterprise. Illimitable prairies had been sown with an Earth-type grass which destroyed the native ground-cover—the reverse of the ground-cover situation here—and the entire planet was a monstrous range for beef cattle. Dotted about were gigantic slaughterhouses, and cattle in masses of tens of thousands were shifted here and there by ground-induction fields which acted as fences. Ultimately the cattle were driven by these same induction fences to the slaughter houses and actually into the chutes where their throats were slit. Every imaginable fraction of a credit of profit was extracted from their carcasses, and Calhoun had found it appalling.

He was not sentimental about cattle, but the complete cold-bloodedness of the entire operation sickened him. The same cold-bloodedness was practised toward the human employees who ran the place. Their living quarters were sub-marginal. The air stank of cattle murder. Men worked for the Texia Company or they did not work. If they did not work they did not eat. If they worked and ate,—Calhoun could see nothing satisfying in being alive on a world like that! His report to Med Service had been biting. He'd been prejudiced against businessmen ever since.

*

But a parachute descended, blowing away from the city. It would land not too far from the highway he followed. And it didn't occur to Calhoun not to help the unknown chutist. He saw a small figure dangling below the chute. He slowed the ground-car as he estimated where the parachute would land.

He was off the twelve-lane highway and on a feeder road when the chute was a hundred feet high. He was racing across a field of olive-green plants that went all the way to the horizon when the parachute actually touched ground. There was a considerable wind. The man in the harness bounced. He didn't know how to spill the air. The chute dragged him.

Calhoun sped ahead, swerved and ran into the chute. He stopped the car and the chute stopped with it. He got out.

The man lay in a hopeless tangle of cordage. He thrust unskilfully at it. When Calhoun came up he said suspiciously:

"Have you a knife?"

Calhoun offered a knife, politely opening its blade. The man slashed at the cords and freed himself. There was an attache case lashed to his chute harness. He cut at those cords. The attache case not only came clear, but opened. It dumped out an incredible mass of brand new, tightly packed interstellar credit certificates. Calhoun could see that the denominations were one thousand and ten thousand credits. The man from the chute reached under his armpit and drew out a blaster.

It was not a service weapon. It was elaborate, practically a toy. With a dour glance at Calhoun he put it in a side pocket and gathered up the scattered money. It was an enormous sum, but he packed it back. He stood up.

"My name is Allison," he said in an authoritative voice. "Arthur Allison. I'm much obliged. Now I'll ask you to take me to Maya City."

"No," said Calhoun politely. "I just left there. It's deserted. I'm not going back. There's nobody there."

"But I've important bus—" The other man stared. "It's deserted? But that's impossible!"

"Quite," agreed Calhoun, "but it's true. It's abandoned. Uninhabited. Everybody's left it. There's no one there at all."

The man who called himself Allison blinked unbelievingly. He swore. Then he raged profanely.

But he was not bewildered by the news. Which, upon consideration, was itself almost bewildering. But then his eyes grew shrewd. He looked about him.

"My name is Allison," he repeated, as if there were some sort of magic in the word. "Arthur Allison. No matter what's happened, I've some business to do here. Where have the people gone? I need to find them."

"I need to find them too," said Calhoun. "I'll take you with me, if you like."

"You've heard of me." It was a statement, confidently made.

"Never," said Calhoun politely. "If you're not hurt, suppose you get in the car? I'm as anxious as you are to find out what's happened. I'm Med Service."

*

Allison moved toward the car.

"Med Service, eh? I don't think much of the Med Service! You people try to meddle in things that are none of your business!"

Calhoun did not answer. The muddy man, clutching the attache case tightly, waded through the olive-green plants to the car and climbed in. Murgatroyd said cordially, *"Chee-chee!"* but Allison viewed him with distaste.

"What's this?"

"He's Murgatroyd," said Calhoun. "He's a *tormal*. He's Med service personnel."

"I don't like beasts," said Allison coldly.

"He's much more important to me than you are," said Calhoun, "if the matter should come to a test."

Allison stared at him as if expecting him to cringe. Calhoun did not. Allison showed every sign of being an important man who expected his importance to be recognized and catered to. When Calhoun stirred impatiently he got into the car and growled a little. Calhoun took his place. The ground-car hummed. It rose on the six columns of air which took the place of wheels and slid across the field of dark-green plants, leaving the parachute deflated across a number of rows, and a trail of crushed-down plants where it had moved.

It reached the highway again. Calhoun ran the car up on the highway's shoulder, and then suddenly checked. He'd noticed something.

He stopped the car and got out. Where the ploughed field ended, and before the coated surface of the highway began, there was a space where on another world one would expect to see green grass.

On this planet grass did not grow; but there would normally be some sort of self-planted vegetation where there was soil and sunshine and moisture. There had been such vegetation here, but now there was only a thin, repellent mass of slimy and decaying foliage. Calhoun bent down to it.

It had a sour, faintly astringent smell of decay. These were the ground-cover plants of Maya of which Calhoun had read. They had motile stems, leaves and flowers, and they had cannibalistic tendencies. They were the local weeds which made it impossible to grow grain for human use upon this world.

And they were dead.

Calhoun straightened up and returned to the car. Plants like this were wilted at the base of the spaceport building, and on another place where there should have been sward. Calhoun had seen a large dead member of the genus in a florist's, that had been growing in a cage before it died. There was a singular coincidence here: humans ran away from something, and something caused the death of a particular genus of cannibal weeds.

MED SHIP MAN

It did not exactly add up to anything in particular, and certainly wasn't evidence for anything at all. But Calhoun drove on in a vaguely puzzled mood. The germ of a guess was forming in his mind. He couldn't pretend to himself that it was likely, but it was surely no more unlikely than most of a million human beings abandoning their homes at a moment's notice.

III

They came to the turnoff for a town called Tenochitlan, some forty miles from Maya City. Calhoun swung off the highway to go through it.

Whoever had chosen the name Maya for this planet had been interested in the legends of Yucatan, back on Earth. There were many instances of such hobbies in a Med Ship's list of ports of call. Calhoun touched ground regularly on planets that had been named for countries and towns when men first roamed the stars, and nostalgically christened their discoveries with names suggested by homesickness. There was a Tralee, and a Dorset, and an Eire. Colonists not infrequently took their world's given name as a pattern and chose related names for seas and peninsulas and mountain chains. On Texia the landing-grid rose near a town called Corral and the principal meat-packing settlement was named Roundup.

Whatever the name Tenochitlan would have suggested, though, was denied by the town itself. It was small, with a pleasing local type of architecture. There were shops and some factories, and many strictly private homes, some clustered close together and others in the middles of considerable gardens. In those gardens also there was wilt and decay among the cannibal plants. There was no grass, because the plants prevented it, but now the motile plants themselves were dead. Except for the one class of killed growing things, however, vegetation was luxuriant.

But the little city was deserted. Its streets were empty, its houses untenanted. Some houses were apparently locked up here, though, and Calhoun saw three or four shops whose stock in trade had been covered over before the owners departed. He guessed that either this town had been warned earlier than the spaceport city, or else they knew they had time to get in motion before the highways were filled with the cars from the west.

Allison looked at the houses with keen, evaluating eyes. He did not seem to notice the absence of people. When Calhoun swung back on the great road beyond the little city, Allison regarded the endless fields of dark-green plants with much the same sort of interest.

"Interesting," he said abruptly when Tenochitlan fell behind and dwindled to a speck. "Very interesting! I'm interested in land. Real property, that's my business. I've a land-owning corporation on Thanet Three. I've some holdings on Dorset, too, and elsewhere. It just occurred to me: what's all this land and the cities worth, with the people all run away?"

"What," asked Calhoun, "are the people worth who've run?"

Allison paid no attention. He looked shrewd. Thoughtful.

"I came here to buy land," he said. "I'd arranged to buy some hundreds of square miles. I'd buy more if the price were right. But—as things are, it looks like the price of land ought to go down quite a bit. Quite a bit!"

"It depends," said Calhoun, "on whether there's anybody left alive to sell it to you, and what sort of thing has happened."

Allison looked at him sharply.

"Ridiculous!" he said authoritatively. "There's no question of their being alive!"

"They thought there might be," observed Calhoun. "That's why they ran away. They hoped they'd be safe where they ran to. I hope they are."

Allison ignored the comment. His eyes remained intent and shrewd. He was not bewildered by the flight of the people of Maya. His mind was busy with contemplation of that flight from the standpoint of a man of business.

*

The car went racing onward. The endless fields of dark green rushed past to the rear. The highway was deserted, just three strips of surfaced road, mathematically straight, going on to the horizon. They went on by tens and scores of miles, each strip wide enough to allow four ground-cars to run side by side. The highway was intended to allow all the produce of all these fields to be taken to market or a processing plant at the highest possible speed and in any imaginable quantity. The same roads had allowed the cities to be deserted instantly the warning—whatever the warning was—arrived.

Fifty miles beyond Tenochitlan there was a mile-long strip of sheds containing agricultural machinery for crop culture and trucks to carry the crops to market. There was no sign of life about the machinery, nor in a further hour's run to westward.

Then there was a city visible to the left. But it was not served by this particular highway, but another. There was no sign of any movement in its streets. It moved along the horizon to the left and rear. Presently it disappeared.

Half an hour later still, Murgatroyd said:

"*Chee!*"

He stirred uneasily. A moment later he said "*Chee!*" again.

Calhoun turned his eyes from the road. Murgatroyd looked unhappy. Calhoun ran his hand over the *tormal*'s furry body. Murgatroyd pressed against him. The car raced on. Murgatroyd whimpered a little. Calhoun's hand felt the little animal's muscles tense sharply, and then relax, and after a little tense again. Murgatroyd said almost hysterically:

"*Chee-chee-chee-chee!*"

Calhoun stopped the car, but Murgatroyd did not seem to be relieved. Allison said impatiently, "What's the matter?"

"That's what I'm trying to find out," said Calhoun.

He felt Murgatroyd's pulse. The role of Murgatroyd in the Med Ship *Esclipus Twenty* was not only that of charming companion in the long, isolated runs in overdrive. Murgatroyd was a part of the Med Service. His tribe had been discovered on a planet in the Deneb sector, and men had made pets of them, to the high satisfaction of the *tormals*. Presently it was discovered that veterinarians never had *tormals* for patients. They were invariably in robustuous good health. They contracted no infections from other animals; they shared no infections with anybody else. The Med Service discovered that *tormals* possessed a dynamic immunity to germ and bacteria-caused diseases. Even viruses injected into their bloodstreams only provoked an immediate, overwhelming development of antibodies, so that *tormals* couldn't be given any known disease. Which was of infinite value to the Med Service.

Now every Med Ship that could be supplied with a *tormal* carried a small, affectionate, whiskered member of the tribe. Men liked them, and they adored men. And when, as sometimes happened, by mutation or the simple enmity of nature, a new kind of infection appeared in human society—why—*tormals* defeated it. They produced specific antibodies to destroy it. Men analyzed the antibodies and synthesized them, and they were available to all the humans who needed them. So a great many millions of humans stayed alive, because *tormals* were pleasant little animals with a precious genetic gift of good health.

*

Calhoun looked at his sweep-second watch, timing the muscular spasms that Murgatroyd displayed. They coincided with irregularities in Murgatroyd's heartbeat, coming at approximately two-second intervals. The tautening of the muscles lasted just about half a second.

"But I don't feel it!" said Calhoun.

Murgatroyd whimpered again and said, "*Chee-chee!*"

"What's going on?" demanded Allison with the impatience of a very important man indeed. "If the beast's sick, he's sick! I've got to find—"

Calhoun opened his med kit and went carefully through it until he found what he needed. He put a pill into Murgatroyd's mouth.

"Swallow it!" he commanded.

Murgatroyd resisted, but the pill went down. Calhoun watched him sharply. Murgatroyd's digestive system was delicate, but it was dependable. Anything that might be poisonous, Murgatroyd's stomach rejected instantly and emphatically.

The pill stayed down.

"Look!" said Allison indignantly. "I've got business to do! In this attache case I have millions of interstellar credits, in cash, to pay down on purchases of land and factories. I ought to make some damned good deals! And I figure that that's as important as anything else you can think of! It's a damned sight more important than a beast with a belly-ache!"

Calhoun looked at him coldly.

"Do you own land on Texia?" he asked.

Allison's mouth dropped open. Extreme suspicion and unease appeared on his face. As a sign of the unease, his hand went to the side coat pocket in which he'd put a blaster. He didn't pluck it out. Calhoun's left fist swung around and landed. He took Allison's elaborate pocket blaster and threw it away among the monotonous rows of olive-green plants. He returned to absorbed observation of Murgatroyd.

In five minutes the muscular spasms diminished. In ten, Murgatroyd frisked. But he seemed to think that Calhoun had done something remarkable. In the warmest of tones he said:

"*Chee!*"

"Very good," said Calhoun. "We'll go ahead. I suspect you'll do as well as we do—for a while."

The car lifted the few inches the air columns sustained it above the ground. It went on, still to the eastward. But Calhoun drove more slowly now.

"Something was giving Murgatroyd rhythmic muscular spasms," he said coldly. "I gave him medication to stop them. He's more sensitive than we are, so he reacted to a stimulus we haven't noticed yet. But I think we'll notice it presently."

Allison seemed to be dazed at the affront given him. It appeared to be unthinkable that anybody might lay hands on him.

"What the devil has that to do with me?" he demanded angrily. "And what did you hit me for? You're going to pay for this!"

"Until I do," Calhoun told him, "you'll be quiet. And it does have the devil to do with you. There was a Med Service gadget once—a tricky little device to produce contraction of chosen muscles. It was useful for re-starting stopped hearts without the need of an operation. It regulated the beat of hearts that were too slow or dangerously irregular. But some businessman had a bright idea and got a tame researcher to link that gadget to ground induction currents. I suspect you know that businessman!"

"I don't know what you're talking about," snapped Allison. But he was singularly tense.

"I do," said Calhoun unpleasantly. "I made a public health inspection on Texia a couple of years ago. The whole planet is a single, gigantic, cattle-raising enterprise. They don't use metal fences—the herds are too big to be stopped by such things. They don't use cowboys—they cost money. On Texia they use ground-induction and the Med Service gadget linked together to serve as cattle fences. They act like fences, though they're projected through the ground. Cattle become uncomfortable when they try to cross them. So they draw back. So men control them. They move them from place to place by changing the cattle fences, which are currents induced in the ground. The cattle have to keep moving or be punished by the moving fence. They're even driven into the slaughterhouse chutes by ground-induction fields! That's the trick on Texia, where induction fields herd cattle. I think it's the trick on Maya, where people are herded like cattle and driven out of their cities so the value of their fields and factories will drop,—so a land buyer can find bargains!"

"You're insane!" snapped Allison. "I just landed on this planet! You saw me land! I don't know what happened before I got here! How could I?"

"You might have arranged it," said Calhoun.

*

Allison assumed an air of offended and superior dignity. Calhoun drove the car onward at very much less than the head-long pace he'd been keeping to. Presently he looked down at his hands on the steering wheel. Now and then the tendons to his fingers seemed to twitch. At rhythmic intervals, the skin crawled on the back of his hands. He glanced at Allison. Allison's hands were tightly clenched.

"There's a ground-induction fence in action, all right," said Calhoun calmly. "You notice? It's a cattle fence and we're running into it. If we were cattle, now, we'd turn around and move away."

"I don't know what you're talking about!" said Allison.

But his hands stayed clenched. Calhoun slowed the car still more. He began to feel, all over his body, that every muscle tended to twitch at the same time. It was a horrible sensation. His heart muscles tended to contract too, simultaneously with the rest, but one's heart has its own beat rate. Sometimes the normal beat coincided with the twitch. Then his heart pounded violently—so violently that it was painful. But equally often the imposed contraction of the heart muscles came just after a normal contraction, and then it stayed tightly knotted for half a second. It missed a beat, and the feeling was agony.

No animal would have pressed forward in the face of such sensations. It would have turned back long ago. No animal. Not even Man.

Calhoun stopped the car. He looked at Murgatroyd. Murgatroyd was completely himself. He looked inquiringly at Calhoun. Calhoun nodded to him, but he spoke—with some difficulty—to Allison.

"We'll see—if this thing—builds up. You know that it's the Texia—trick. A ground-induction unit set up—here. It drove people—like cattle. Now we've—run into it.—It's holding people—like cattle."

25

He panted. His chest muscles contracted with the rest, so that his breathing was interfered with. But Murgatroyd, who'd been made uneasy and uncomfortable before Calhoun noticed anything wrong, was now bright and frisky. Medication had desensitized his muscles to outside stimuli. He would be able to take a considerable electric shock without responding to it.

But he could be killed by one that was strong enough.

A savage anger filled Calhoun. Everything fitted together. Allison had put his hand convenient to his blaster when Calhoun mentioned Texia. It meant that Calhoun suspected what Allison knew to be true. A cattle-fence unit had been set up on Maya, and it was holding—like cattle—the people it had previously driven—like cattle. Calhoun could deduce with some precision exactly what had been done. The first experience of Maya with the cattle fence would have been very mild. It would have been low-power, causing just enough uneasiness to be noticed. It would have moved from west to east, slowly, and it would have reached a certain spot and there faded out. And it would have been a mystery and an uncomfortable thing, and nobody would understand it on Maya. In a week it would almost be forgotten. But then there'd come a stronger disturbance. And it would travel like the first one; down the length of the peninsula on which the colony lay, but stopping at the same spot as before, and then fading away to nothingness. And this also would have seemed mysterious. But nobody would suspect humans of causing it. There would be theorizing and much questioning, but it would be considered an unfamiliar natural event.

Probably the third use of the cattle fence would be most disturbing. This time it would be acutely painful. But it would move into the cities and through them and past them, and it would go down the peninsula to where it had stopped and faded on two previous occasions.

The people of Maya would be disturbed and scared. But they considered that they knew it began to the westward of Maya City, and moved toward the east at such-and-such a speed, and it went so far and no farther. And they would organize themselves to apply this carefully worked out information.

It would not occur to any of them that they had learned how to be driven like cattle.

*

Calhoun, of course, could only reason that this must have happened. But nothing else could have taken place. Perhaps there were more than three uses of the moving cattle fence to get the people prepared to move past the known place at which it always faded to nothingness. They might have been days apart, or weeks apart, or months. There might have been stronger manifestations followed by weaker ones and then stronger ones again.

But there was an inductive cattle fence across the highway here. Calhoun had driven into it. Every two seconds the muscles of his body tensed. Sometimes his heart missed a beat at the time that his breathing stopped, and sometimes it pounded violently. It seemed that the symptoms became more and more unbearable.

He got out his med kit, with hands that spasmodically jerked uncontrollably. He fumbled out the same medication he'd given Murgatroyd. He took two of the pellets.

"In reason," he said coldly, "I ought to let you take what this damned thing would give you. But—here!"

Allison had panicked. The *idea* of a cattle fence suggested discomfort, of course, but it did not imply danger. The *experience* of a cattle fence, designed for huge hoofed beasts instead of men, was terrifying. Allison gasped. He made convulsive movements. Calhoun himself moved erratically. For one and a half seconds out of two, he could control his muscles. For half a second at a time, he could not. But he poked a pill into Allison's mouth.

"Swallow it!" he commanded. "Swallow!"

The ground-car rested tranquilly on the highway, which here went on for a mile and then dipped in a gentle incline and then rose once more. The totally level fields to right and left came to an end here. Native trees grew, trailing preposterously with long fronds. Brushwood hid much of the ground. That looked normal. But the lower, ground-covering vegetation was wilted and rotting.

Allison choked upon the pellet. Calhoun forced a second upon him. Murgatroyd looked inquisitively at first one and then the other of the two men. He said:

"*Chee? Chee?*"

Calhoun lay back in his seat, breathing carefully to keep alive. But he couldn't do anything about his heartbeat. The sun shone brightly, though now it was low, toward the horizon. There were clouds in the reddened sky. A gentle breeze blew. Everything, to outward appearance, was peaceful and tranquil and commonplace upon this small world.

But in the area that human beings had taken over there were cities which were still and silent and deserted, and somewhere—somewhere!—the population of the planet waited uneasily for the latest of a series of increasingly terrifying phenomena to come to an end. Up to this time the strange, creeping, universal affliction had begun at one place, and moved slowly to another, and then diminished and ceased to be. But this was the greatest and worst of the torments. And it hadn't ended. It hadn't diminished. After three days it continued at full strength at the place where previously it had stopped and died away.

The people of Maya were frightened. They couldn't return to their homes. They couldn't go anywhere. They hadn't prepared for an emergency to last for days. They hadn't brought supplies of food.

It began to look as if they were going to starve.

IV

Calhoun was in very bad shape when the sports car came to the end of the highway.

First, all the multiple roadways of the route that had brought him here were joined by triple ribbons of road-surface from the north. For a space there were twenty-four lanes available to traffic. They flowed together, and then there were twelve. Here there was evidence of an enormous traffic concentration at some time now past. Brush and small trees were crushed and broken where cars had been forced to travel off the hard-surface roadways and through undergrowth. The twelve lanes dwindled to six, and the unpaved area on either side showed that innumerable cars had been forced to travel off the highway altogether. Then there were three lanes, and then two, and finally only a single ribbon of pavement where no more than two cars could run side by side. The devastation on either hand was astounding. All visible vegetation for half a mile to right and left was crushed and tangled. And then the narrow surfaced road ceased to be completely straight. It curved around a hillock—and here the ground was no longer perfectly flat—and came to an end.

And Calhoun saw all the ground-cars of the planet gathered and parked together.

There were no buildings. There were no streets. There was nothing of civilization but tens and scores of thousands of ground-cars. They were extraordinary to look at, stopped at random, their fronts pointed in all directions, their air-column tubes thrusting into the ground so that there might be trouble getting them clear again.

Parked bumper to bumper in closely placed lines, in theory twenty-five thousand cars could be parked on a square mile of ground. But there were very many times that number of cars here, and some places were unsuitable for parking, and there were lanes placed at random and there'd been no special effort to put the maximum number of cars in the smallest place. So the surface transportation system of the planet Maya spread out over some fifty sprawling square miles. Here, cars were crowded closely. There, there was much room between them. But it seemed that as far as one could see in the twilight there were glistening vehicles gathered confusedly, so there was nothing else to be seen but an occasional large tree rising from among them.

Calhoun came to the end of the surfaced road. He'd waited for the pellets he'd taken and given to Allison to have the effect they'd had on Murgatroyd. That had come about. He'd driven on. But the strength of the inductor field had increased to the intolerable. When he stopped the sports car he showed the effects of what he'd been through.

Figures on foot converged upon him instantly. There were eager calls.

"It's stopped? You got through? We can go back?"

Calhoun shook his head. It was just past sunset and many brilliant colorings showed in the western sky, but they couldn't put color into Calhoun's face. His cheeks were grayish and his eyes were deep-sunk, and he looked like someone in the last stages of exhaustion. He said heavily:

"It's still there. We came through. I'm Med Service. Have you got a government here? I need to talk to somebody who can give orders."

*

If he'd asked two days earlier there would have been no answer, because the fugitives were only waiting for a disaster to come to an end. One day earlier, he might have found men with authority busily trying to arrange for drinking water for something like two millions of people, in the entire absence of wells or pumps or ways of making either. And if he'd been a day later, it is rather likely that he'd have found savage disorder. But he arrived at sundown three days after the flight from the cities. There was no food to speak of, and water was drastically short, and the fugitives were only beginning to suspect that they would never be able to leave this place—and that they might die here.

Men left the growing crowd about the sports car to find individuals who could give orders. Calhoun stayed in the car, resting from the unbearable strain he'd undergone. The ground-inductor cattle fence had been ten miles deep. One mile was not bad. Only Murgatroyd had noticed it. After two miles Calhoun and Allison suffered; but the medication strengthened them to take it. But there'd been a long, long way in the center of the induction-field in which existence was pure torment. Calhoun's muscles defied him for part of every two-second cycle, and his heart and lungs seemed constantly about to give up even the pretense of working. In that part of the cattle-fence field, he'd hardly dared drive faster than a crawl, in order to keep control of the car when his own body was uncontrollable. But presently the field strength lessened and ultimately ended.

Now Murgatroyd looked cordially at the figures who clustered about the car. He'd hardly suffered at all. He'd had half as much of the medication as Calhoun himself, and his body weight was only a tenth of Calhoun's. He'd made out all right. Now he looked expectantly at what became a jammed mass of crowding men about the vehicle that had come through the invisible barrier across the highway. They hoped desperately for news to produce hope. But Murgatroyd waited zestfully for somebody to welcome him and offer him cakes and sweets, and undoubtedly presently a cup of coffee.

But nobody did.

It was a long time before there was a stirring at the edge of the crowd. Night had fully fallen then, and for miles and miles in all directions lights in the ground cars of Maya's inhabitants glowed brightly. They drew upon broadcast power, naturally, for their motors and their lights. Off to one side someone shouted. Calhoun turned on his headlights for a guide. More shoutings. A knot of men struggled to get through the crowd. With difficulty, presently, they reached the car.

"They say you got through," panted a tall man, "but you can't get back. They say—"

Calhoun roused himself. Allison, beside him, stirred. The tall man panted again:

"I'm the planetary president. What can we do?"

"First, listen," said Calhoun tiredly.

He'd had a little rest. Not much, but some. The actual work he'd done in driving three hundred-odd miles from Maya City was trivial. But the continuous, and lately violent, spasms of his heart and breathing muscles had been exhausting. He heard Murgatroyd say ingratiatingly, "*Chee-chee-chee-chee,*" and put his hand on the little animal to quiet him.

"The thing you ran away from," said Calhoun with effort, "is a type of ground-induction field using broadcast power from the grid. It's used on Texia to confine cattle to their pastures and to move them where they're wanted to be. But it was designed for cattle. It's a cattle fence. It could kill humans."

*

He went on, his voice gaining strength and steadiness as he spoke. He explained, precisely, how a ground-induction field was projected in a line at a right angle to its source. It could be moved by adjustments of the apparatus by which it was projected.

"But—but if it uses broadcast power," the planetary president said urgently, "then if the power broadcast is cut off it has to stop! If you got through it coming here, tell us how to get through going back and we'll cut off the power broadcast ourselves! We've got to do something immediately. The whole planet's here. There's no food! There's no water! Something has to be done before we begin to die!"

"But," said Calhoun, "if you cut off the power you'll die anyway! You've got a couple of million people here, and you're a hundred miles from food. Without power you couldn't get to food or bring it here. Cut the power and you're still stranded here. Without power you'll die as soon as with it."

There was a sound from the listening men around. It was partly a growl and partly a groan.

"I've just found this out," said Calhoun. "I didn't know until the last ten miles exactly what the situation was, and I had to come here to be sure. Now I need some people to help me. It won't be pleasant. I may have enough medication to get a dozen people back through. It'll be safer if I take only six. Get a doctor to pick me six men. Good heart action. Sound lungs. Two should be electronics engineers. The others should be good shots. If you get them ready, I'll give them the same stuff that got us through. It's desensitizing medication, but it will do only so much. And try and find some weapons for them."

Voices murmured all around. Men hastily explained to other men what Calhoun had said. The creeping disaster before which they'd all fled,—it was not a natural catastrophe, but an artificial one! Men had made it! They'd been herded here and their wives and children were hungry because of something men had done!

A low-pitched, buzzing, humming sound came from the crowd about the sports car. For the moment, nobody asked what could be the motive for men to do what had been done. Pure fury filled the mob. Calhoun leaned closer to Allison.

"I wouldn't get out of the car if I were you," he said in a low tone. "I certainly wouldn't try to buy any real property at a low price!"

Allison shivered. There was a vast, vast stirring as the explanation passed from man to man. Figures moved away in the darkness. Lighted car windows winked as they moved through the obscurity. The population of Maya was spread out over very many square miles of what had been wilderness, and there was no elaborate communication system by which information could be spread quickly. But long before dawn there'd be nobody who didn't know that they'd fled from a man-made danger and were held here like cattle, behind a cattle fence, apparently abandoned to die.

*

Allison's teeth chattered. He was a business man and up to now he'd thought as one. He'd made decisions in offices, with attorneys and secretaries and clerks to make the decisions practical and safe, without any concern for any consequences other than financial ones.

He saw possible consequences to himself, here and now. He'd landed on Maya because he considered the matter too important to trust to anybody else. Even riding with Calhoun on the way here, he'd only been elated and astonished at the success of the intended coup. He'd raised his aim. For a while he'd believed that he'd end as the sole proprietor of the colony on Maya, with every plant growing for his profit, and every factory earning money for him, and every inhabitant his employee. It had been the most grandiose possible dream. The details and the maneuvers needed to complete it flowed into his mind.

But now his teeth chattered. At ten words from Calhoun he would literally be torn to pieces by the raging men about him. His attache case with millions of credits in cash—it would be proof of whatever Calhoun chose to say. Allison knew terror down to the bottom of his soul. But he dared not move from Calhoun's side, even though a single sentence in the calmest of voices would destroy him, and he'd never faced actual, understood, physical danger before.

Presently men came, one by one, to take orders from Calhoun. They were able-bodied and grim-faced men. Two were electronics engineers, as he'd specified. One was a policeman. There were two mechanics and a doctor who was also amateur tennis champion of the planet. Calhoun doled out to them the pellets that reduced the sensitiveness of muscles to externally applied stimuli. He gave instructions. They'd go as far into the cattle fence as they could reasonably endure. Then they'd swallow the pellets and let them act. Then they'd go on. His stock of pellets was limited. He could give three to each man.

Murgatroyd squirmed disappointedly as this briefing went on. Obviously, he wasn't to make a social success here. He was annoyed, and he needed more space. Calhoun tossed Allison's attache case behind the seats. Allison was too terrified to protest. It still did not increase the space left on the front seat between Calhoun and Allison.

Four humming ground cars lifted eight inches off the ground and hovered there on columns of rushing air. Calhoun took the lead. His headlights moved down the single-lane road to which two joining twelve-lane highways had shrunk. Behind him, other headlights moved into line. Calhoun's car moved away into the darkness. The others followed.

Brilliant stars shone overhead. A cluster of thousands of suns, a hundred light-years away, made a center of illumination that gave Maya's night the quality of a vivid if diffused moonlight. The cars went on. Presently

Calhoun felt the twitchings of minor muscular spasms. He was riding into the field which had been first devised for purposes remote from the herding of cattle or humans, but applied to the first use on the planet Texia, and now applied to the second here.

The road became two, and then four, and then eight lanes wide. Then four lanes swirled off to one side, and the remaining four presently doubled, and then widened again, and it was the twelve-lane turnpike that had brought Calhoun here from Maya City.

*

But the rhythmic interference with his body grew stronger. Allison had spoken not one single word while Calhoun conferred with the people of Maya beyond the highway. His teeth chattered as they started back. He didn't attempt to speak during the beginning of the ride through the cattle-fence field. His teeth chattered, and stopped, and chattered again, and at long last he panted despairingly:

"Are you going to let the thing kill me?"

Calhoun stopped. The cars behind him stopped. He gave Allison two pellets and took two himself. With Murgatroyd insistently accompanying him, he went along the cars which trailed him. He made sure the six men he'd asked for took their pellets and that they had an adequate effect. He went back to the sports car.

Allison whimpered a little when he and Murgatroyd got back in.

"I thought," said Calhoun conversationally, "that you might try to take off by yourself, just now. It would solve a problem for me. Of course it wouldn't solve any for you. But I don't think your problems have any solution, now."

He started the car up again. It moved forward. The other cars trailed dutifully. They went on through the starlit night. Calhoun noted that the effect of the cattle fence was less than it had been before. The first desensitizing pellets had not wholly lost their effect when he added to it. But he kept his speed low until he was certain the other drivers had endured the anguish of passing through the cattle-fence field.

Presently he was confident that the cattle field was past. He sent his car up to eighty miles an hour. The other cars followed faithfully. To a hundred. They did not drop behind. The car hummed through the night at top speed—a hundred and twenty, a hundred and thirty miles an hour. The three other cars' headlights faithfully kept pace with him.

Allison, said desperately, "Look! I—don't understand what's happened. You talk as if I'd planned all this. I—did have advance notice of a—a research project here. But it shouldn't have held the people there for days! Something went wrong! I only believed that people would want to leave Maya. I'd only planned to buy as much acreage as I could, and control of as many factories as possible. That's all! It was business! Only business!"

Calhoun did not answer. Allison might be telling the truth. Some businessmen would think it only intelligent to frighten people into selling their holdings below true value. Something of the sort happened every day in stock exchanges. But the people of Maya could have died!

For that matter, they still might. They couldn't return to their homes and food so long as broadcast power kept the cattle-fence in existence. But they could not return to their homes and food supplies if the power broadcast was cut off, either.

Over all the night surface of the world of Maya there was light only on one highway at one spot, and a multitude of smaller, lesser lights where the people of Maya waited to find out whether they would live or die.

V

Calhoun considered coldly. They were beyond what had been the farthest small city on the multiple highway. They would go on past now-starlit fields of plants native to Maya, passing many places where trucks loaded with the plants climbed up to the roadway and headed for the factories which made use of them. The fields ran for scores of miles along the highway's length. They reached out beyond the horizon,—perhaps scores of miles in that direction, too. There were thousands upon thousands of square miles devoted to the growing of the dark-green vegetation which supplied the raw materials for Maya's space exports. Some hundred-odd miles ahead, the small town of Tenochitlan lay huddled in the light of the distant star-cluster. Beyond that, more highway and Maya City. Beyond that—

Calhoun reasoned that the projector to make the induction cattle fence would be beyond Maya City, somewhere in the mountains the photograph in the spaceport building showed. A large highway went into those mountains for a limited distance only.

A ground-inductor projector field always formed at a right angle to the projector which was its source. It could be adjusted—the process was analogous to focusing—to come into actual being at any distance desired, and the distance could be changed. To drive the people of Maya City eastward, the projector of a cattle fence—about which they would know nothing; it would be totally strange and completely mysterious—the projector of the cattle fence would need to be west of the people to be driven. Logically, it would belong in the mountains. Practically, it would be concealed. Drawing on broadcast power to do its work, there would be no large power source needed to give it the six million kilowatts it required. It should be quite easy to hide beyond any quick or easy discovery. Hunting it out might require weeks of searching.

But the people beyond the end of the highway couldn't wait. They had no food, and holes scrabbled down to ground-water by men digging with their bare hands simply would not be adequate. The cattle fence had to be cut off immediately—while the broadcast of power had to be continued.

Calhoun made an abrupt grunting noise. Phrasing the thing that needed to be done was practically a blueprint of how to do it. Simple! He'd need the two electronics engineers, of course. But that would be the trick....

He drove on at a hundred thirty miles an hour with his lips set wrily. The three other cars came behind him. Murgatroyd watched the way ahead. Mile after mile, half-minute after half-minute, the headlights cast brilliantly blinding beams before the cars. Murgatroyd grew bored. He said, "*Chee!*" in a discontented fashion and tried to curl up between Allison and Calhoun. There wasn't room. He crawled over the seat-back. He moved about, back there. There were rustling sounds. He settled down. Presently there was silence. Undoubtedly he had draped his furry tail across his nose and gone soundly off to sleep.

Allison spoke suddenly. He'd had time to think, but he had no practice in various ways of thinking.

"How much money have you got?" he asked.

"Not much," said Calhoun. "Why?"

"I—haven't done anything illegal," said Allison, with an unconvincing air of confidence, "but I could be put to some inconvenience if you were to accuse me before others of what you've accused me personally. You seem to think that I planned a criminal act. That the action I know of—the research project I'd heard of—that it became—that it got out of hand is likely. But I am entirely in the clear. I did nothing in which I did not have the advice of counsel. I am legally unassailable. My lawyers—"

*

"That's none of my business," Calhoun told him. "I'm a medical man. I landed here in the middle of what seemed to be a serious public health situation. I went to see what had happened. I've found out. I still haven't the answer,—not the whole answer anyway. But the human population of Maya is in a state of some privation, not to say danger. I hope to end it. But I've nothing to do with anybody's guilt or innocence of crime or criminal intent or anything else."

Allison swallowed. Then he said with smooth confidence:

"But you could cause me inconvenience. I would appreciate it if you would—would—"

"Cover up what you've done?" asked Calhoun.

"No! I've done nothing wrong. But you could simply use discretion. I landed by parachute to complete some business deals I'd arranged months ago. I will go through with them. I will leave on the next ship. That's perfectly open and above board. Strictly business. But you could make a—an unpleasing public image of me. Yet I have done nothing any other business man wouldn't do! I did happen to know of a research project—"

"I think," said Calhoun without heat, "that you sent men here with a cattle-fence device from Texia to frighten the people on Maya. They wouldn't know what was going on. They'd be scared; they'd want to get away. So you'd be able to buy up practically all the colony for the equivalent of peanuts. I can't prove that," he conceded, "but that's my opinion. But you want me not to state it. Is that right?"

"Exactly!" said Allison. He'd been shaken to the core, but he managed the tone and the air of a dignified man of business discussing an unpleasant subject with fine candor. "I assure you you are mistaken. You agree that you can't prove your suspicions. If you can't prove them, you shouldn't state them. That is simple ethics. You agree to that!"

Calhoun looked at him curiously.

"Are you waiting for me to tell you my price?"

"I'm waiting," said Allison reprovingly, "for you to agree not to cause me embarrassment. I won't be ungrateful. After all, I'm a person of some influence. I could do a great deal to your benefit. I'd be glad—"

"Are you working around to guess at a price I'll take?" asked Calhoun with the same air of curiosity.

He seemed much more curious than indignant, and much more amused than curious. Allison sweated suddenly. Calhoun didn't appear to be bribable. But Allison knew desperation.

"If you want to put it that way—yes," he said harshly. "You can name your own figure. I mean it!"

"I won't say a word about you," said Calhoun. "I won't need to. The characters who're operating your cattle fence will do all the talking that's necessary. Things all fit together,—except for one item. They've been dropping into place all the while we've been driving down this road."

"I said you can name your own figure!" Allison's voice was shrill. "I mean it! Any figure! Any!"

Calhoun shrugged.

"What would a Med Ship man do with money? Forget it!"

He drove on. The highway turnoff to Tenochitlan appeared. Calhoun went steadily past it. The other connection with the road through the town appeared. He left it behind.

Allison's teeth chattered again.

The buildings of Maya City began to appear, some twenty minutes later. Calhoun slowed and the other cars closed up. He opened a window and called:

"We want to go to the landing-grid first. Somebody lead the way!"

A car went past and guided the rest assuredly to a ramp down from the now-elevated road, and through utterly dark streets, of which some were narrow and winding, and came out abruptly where the landing-grid rose skyward. At the bottom its massive girders looked huge and cyclopean in the starlight, but the higher courses looked like silver lace against the stars.

*

They went to the control building. Calhoun got out. Murgatroyd hopped out after him, dust clinging to his fur. He shook himself, and a ten-thousand-credit interstellar credit certificate fell to the ground. Murgatroyd had made a soft place for sleeping out of the contents of

Allison's attache case. It was assuredly the most expensive if not the most comfortable sleeping cushion a *tormal* ever had. Allison sat still as if numbed. He did not even pick up the certificate.

"I need you two electronics men," said Calhoun. Then he said apologetically to the others, "I only figured out something on the way here. I'd believed we might have to take some drastic action, come daybreak. But now I doubt it. I do suggest, though, that you turn off the car headlights and get set to do some shooting if anybody turns up. I don't know whether they will or not."

He led the way inside. He turned on lights. He went to the place where dials showed the amount of power actually being used of the enormous amount available. Those dials now showed an extremely small power drain, considering that the cities of a planet depended on the grid. But the cities were dark and empty of people. The demand needle wavered back and forth, rhythmically. Every two seconds the demand for power went up by six million kilowatts, approximately. The demand lasted for half a second, and stopped. For a second and a half the power in use was reduced by six million kilowatts. During this period only automatic pumps and ventilators and freezing equipment drew on the broadcast power for energy. Then the six-million-kilowatt demand came again for half a second.

"The cattle fence," said Calhoun, "works for half a second out of every two seconds. It's intermittent or it would simply paralyze animals that wandered into it. Or people. Being intermittent, it drives them out instead. There'll be tools and parts for equipment here, in case something needs repair. I want you to make something new."

The two electronics technicians asked questions.

"We need," said Calhoun, "an interruptor that will cut off the power broadcast for the half-second the ground-induction field is supposed to be on. Then it should turn on the broadcast power for the second and a half the cattle fence is supposed to be off. That will stop the cattle-fence effect, and I think a ground car should be able to work with power that's available for three half-seconds out of four."

The electronics men blinked at him. Then they grinned and set to work. Calhoun went exploring. He found a lunch box in a desk with three very stale sandwiches in it. He offered them around.

It appeared that nobody wanted to eat while their families—at the end of the highway—were still hungry.

The electronics men called on the two mechanics to help build something. They explained absorbedly to Calhoun that they were making a cutoff which would adjust to any sudden six-million-kilowatt demand, no matter what time interval was involved. A change in the tempo of the cattle-fence cycle wouldn't bring it back on.

"That's fine!" said Calhoun. "I wouldn't have thought of that!"

He bit into a stale sandwich and went outside. Allison sat limply, despairingly, in his seat in the car.

"The cattle fence is going off," said Calhoun without triumph. "The people of the city will probably begin to get here around sunrise."

"I—I did nothing legally wrong!" said Allison, dry-throated. "Nothing! They'd have to prove that I knew what the—consequences of the research project would be. That couldn't be proved! It couldn't! So I've done nothing legally wrong...."

Calhoun went inside, observing that the doctor who was also tennis champion, and the policeman who'd come to help him, were keeping keen eyes on the city and the foundations of the grid and all other places from which trouble might come.

There was a fine atmosphere of achievement in the power-control room. The power itself did not pass through these instruments, but relays here controlled buried massive conductors which supplied the world with power. And one of the relays had been modified. When the cattle-fence projector closed its circuit, the power went off. When the ground-inductor went off, the power went on. There was no longer a barrier across the highways leading to the east. It was more than probable that ground cars could run on current supplied for one and a half seconds out of every two. They might run jerkily, but they would run.

*

Half an hour later, the amount of power drawn from the broadcast began to rise smoothly and gradually. It could mean only that cars were beginning to move.

Forty-five minutes later still, Calhoun heard stirrings outside. He went out. The two men on guard gazed off into the city. Something moved there. It was a ground-car, running slowly and without lights. Calhoun said undisturbedly:

"Whoever was running the cattle fence found out their gadget wasn't working. Their lights flickered, too. They came to see what was the matter at the landing-grid. But they've seen the lighted windows. Got your blasters handy?"

But the unlighted car turned and raced away. Calhoun only shrugged.

"They haven't a prayer," he said. "We'll take over their apparatus as soon as it's light. It'll be too big to destroy, and there'll be fingerprints and such to identify them as the men who ran it. And they're not natives. When the police start to look for the strangers who were living where the cattle-fence projector was set up.... They can go into the jungles where there's nothing to eat, or they can give themselves up."

He moved toward the door of the control building once more. Allison said desperately:

"They'll have hidden their equipment. You'll never be able to find it!"

Calhoun shook his head in the starlight.

"Anything that can fly can spot it in minutes. Even on the ground one can walk almost straight to it. You see, something happened they didn't count on. That's why they've left it turned on at full power. The earlier, teasing uses of the cattle fence were low-power. Annoying, to start with, and uncomfortable the second time, and maybe somewhat painful the third. But the last time it was full power."

He shrugged. He didn't feel like a long oration. But it was obvious. Something had killed the plants of a certain genus of which small species were weeds that destroyed Earth-type grasses. The ground-cover plants—and the larger ones, like the one Calhoun had seen decaying in a florist's shop which had had to be grown in a cage—the ground-cover plants had motile stems and leaves and blossoms. They were cannibals. They could move their stems to reach, and their leaves to enclose, and their flowers to devour other plants, even perhaps small animals. The point, though, was that they had some limited power of motion. Earth-style sensitive vines and flycatcher plants had primitive muscular tissues. The local ground-cover plants had them too. And the cattle-fence field made those tissues contract spasmodically. Powerfully. Violently. Repeatedly. Until they died of exhaustion. The full-power cattle-fence field had exterminated Mayan ground-cover plants all the way to the end of the east-bound highway. And inevitably—and very conveniently—also up to the exact spot where the cattle-fence field had begun to be projected. There would be an arrow-shaped narrowing of the wiped-out ground-cover plants where the cattle-field had been projected. It would narrow to a point which pointed precisely to the cattle-fence projector.

"Your friends," said Calhoun, "will probably give themselves up and ask for mercy. There's not much else they can do."

Then he said:

"They might even get it. D'you know, there's an interesting side effect of the cattle fence. It kills the plants that have kept Earth-type grasses from growing here. Wheat can be grown here now, whenever and as much as the people please. It should make this a pretty prosperous planet, not having to import all its bread."

*

The ground cars of the inhabitants of Maya City did begin to arrive at sunrise. Within an hour after daybreak, very savagely intent persons found the projector and turned it off.

By noon there was still some anger on the faces of the people of Maya, but there'd been little or no damage, and life took up its normal course again. Murgatroyd appreciated the fact that things went back to normal. For him it was normal to be welcomed and petted when the Med Ship *Esclipus Twenty* touched ground. It was normal for him to move zestfully in admiring human society, and to drink coffee with great gusto.

And while Murgatroyd moved in human society, enjoying himself hugely, Calhoun went about his business. Which, of course, was conferences with planetary health officials, politely receiving such information as they thought important, and tactfully telling them about the most recent developments in medical science.

What else was a Med Ship man for?